D1055572

The Cam Jansen Series

Cam Jansen and the Mystery of the Stolen Diamonds
Cam Jansen and the Mystery of the U.F.O.
Cam Jansen and the Mystery of the Dinosaur Bones
Cam Jansen and the Mystery of the Television Dog
Cam Jansen and the Mystery of the Gold Coins
Cam Jansen and the Mystery of the Babe Ruth Baseball
Cam Jansen and the Mystery of the Circus Clown
Cam Jansen and the Mystery of the Monster Movie
Cam Jansen and the Mystery of the Carnival Prize
Cam Jansen and the Mystery at the Monkey House
Cam Jansen and the Mystery of the Stolen Corn Popper
Cam Jansen and the Mystery of Flight 54
Cam Jansen and the Mystery at the Haunted House
Cam Jansen and the Chocolate Fudge Mystery
Cam Jansen and the Triceratops Pops Mystery
Cam Jansen and the Ghostly Mystery
Cam Jansen and the Scary Snake Mystery
Cam Jansen and the Catnapping Mystery
Cam Jansen and the Barking Treasure Mystery
Cam Jansen and the Birthday Mystery
Cam Jansen and the School Play Mystery
Cam Jansen and the First Day of School Mystery
Cam Jansen and the Tennis Trophy Mystery
Cam Jansen and the Snowy Day Mystery
Cam Jansen and the Valentine Baby Mystery—25th Anniversary Special
Cam Jansen and the Secret Service Mystery
Cam Jansen and the Summer Camp Mysteries—A Super Special

Young Cam Jansen and the Dinosaur Game
Young Cam Jansen and the Missing Cookie
Young Cam Jansen and the Lost Tooth
Young Cam Jansen and the Ice Skate Mystery
Young Cam Jansen and the Baseball Mystery
Young Cam Jansen and the Pizza Shop Mystery
Young Cam Jansen and the Library Mystery
Young Cam Jansen and the Double Beach Mystery
Young Cam Jansen and the Zoo Note Mystery
Young Cam Jansen and the New Girl Mystery
Young Cam Jansen and the Substitute Mystery
Young Cam Jansen and the Spotted Cat Mystery

Cam Jansen

and the
Triceratops Pops
Mystery

David A. Adler

Illustrated by
Susanna Natti

VIKING

VIKING
Published by Penguin Group
Penguin Young Readers Group, 345 Hudson Street, New York, New York 10014, U.S.A.
Penguin Group (Canada), 90 Eglinton Avenue East, Suite 700, Toronto, Ontario,
Canada M4P 2Y3 (a division of Pearson Penguin Canada Inc.)
Penguin Books Ltd, 80 Strand, London WC2R 0RL, England
Penguin Ireland, 25 St Stephen's Green, Dublin 2, Ireland
(a division of Penguin Books Ltd)
Penguin Group (Australia), 250 Camberwell Road, Camberwell,
Victoria 3124, Australia (a division of Pearson Australia Group Pty Ltd)
Penguin Books India Pvt Ltd, 11 Community Centre,
Panchsheel Park, New Delhi – 110 017, India
Penguin Group (NZ), Cnr Airborne and Rosedale Roads, Albany, Auckland 1310,
New Zealand (a division of Pearson New Zealand Ltd)
Penguin Books (South Africa) (Pty) Ltd, 24 Sturdee Avenue, Rosebank,
Johannesburg 2196, South Africa

Penguin Books Ltd, Registered Offices: 80 Strand, London WC2R 0RL, England

First published in 1995 by Viking, a division of Penguin Books USA Inc.

1 3 5 7 9 10 8 6 4 2

Text copyright © David A. Adler, 1995
Illustrations copyright © Susanna Natti, 1995
All rights reserved

LIBRARY OF CONGRESS CATALOGING-IN-PUBLICATION DATA
Adler, David A.
Cam Jansen and the Triceratops Pops mystery / David A. Adler ;
illustrated by Susanna Natti.   p.   cm.—(A Cam Jansen adventure)
Summary: When Cam Jansen and her friend Eric go to the music
store at the mall for the latest CD by the Triceratops Pops band,
Cam uses her photographic memory to foil a crime.
ISBN 978-0-670-86027-2
[1. Mystery and detective stories. 2. Memory—Fiction. 3. Compact discs—Fiction.]
I. Natti, Susanna, ill. II. Title. III. Series: Adler, David A. Cam Jansen adventure.
PZ7.A2615Car 1995 [Fic]—dc20   95-4576 CIP AC

Manufactured in China
Set in Baskerville

For my son Eitan,
who is just learning
to read

Chapter One

Honk! Honk!

A clown sitting on a huge tricycle honked his horn. Then he handed Eric Shelton a flyer.

"Thank you," Eric said.

Someone dressed in a large frog costume handed him another flyer.

"Thank you," Eric said to the frog.

"Ribbit. Ribbit," the frog answered.

"Put your hands in your pockets," Cam told Eric. "If you don't people will keep giving you papers."

Cam Jansen and her friend Eric Shelton were walking through the Hamilton shopping mall. It was a sale day, and the mall was crowded.

"Listen to this," Eric said. He read from one of the flyers. "Today only! Big sale at Jason's Sneaker Palace. You'll run faster in Jason's sneakers."

Then Eric read from the second flyer.

"Today only! Free sprinkles, nuts, and syrup on any two-scoop ice cream cone at Mama Minnie's Sweet Shop."

"I get interesting things in the mail, not at the mall," Cam said. She gave Eric a card. "Listen to what Aunt Molly sent to me."

Cam closed her eyes and said, *"Click."* Cam always says *"Click"* when she wants to remember something.

Cam recited the poem that was printed on the card:

> "I love giraffes and elephants,
> chickens, ducks, and geese,
> but not as much as I love
> my eight-year-old niece.
> Happy Birthday."

"That's silly," Eric said. "You're not eight years old. You're ten."

Cam opened her eyes and said, "And it's not my birthday. That was four months ago."

Cam smiled, and said, "Aunt Molly is nice but very forgetful."

Cam closed her eyes again and told Eric, "Now look on the back of the card. There's a smiling hen sitting on an egg. In the egg is the number 125-98976. That's the number of the card."

"You're right," Eric said. "You have an amazing memory."

Cam has a photographic memory. She remembers just about everything she sees. It's as if she has photographs stored in her head.

Cam's real name is Jennifer. When she was a baby, people called her "Red" because she has red hair. But when they found out about her amazing memory they began calling her "The Camera." Soon "The Camera" was shortened to "Cam."

"There was money inside the card," Cam said. "Aunt Molly wrote that I should buy myself something for my birthday. That's why I'm looking for the music store."

Someone in a rabbit costume gave Eric a flyer.

"Thank you," Eric said to the rabbit.

Eric read from the flyer. "Hoppy news! There's a pajama and sock sale at Benders."

Cam started walking quickly through the shopping mall. Eric had to hurry to keep up.

"Let's get pajamas, or a pair of Jason's sneakers," Eric said, "or some of Mama Minnie's ice cream. I love ice cream with sprinkles."

Cam said, "No, I want to get the new Triceratops Pops CD. I heard one of the songs. It was great."

"I'd rather have ice cream," Eric said. "Close your eyes," he told Cam, "and imagine strawberry ice cream covered with chocolate syrup. Now imagine red, blue, yellow, and green sprinkles sinking into the syrup. On top of all that are walnuts, sliced almonds, and pecans."

Cam closed her eyes. She imagined Eric's

ice cream sundae. And she walked right into a man carrying two large shopping bags. Apples and oranges fell from one of the bags.

Cam opened her eyes and said, "I'm sorry." Then she and Eric chased after the rolling fruit and returned it to the man.

Cam told Eric, "I'm not imagining ice cream anymore. It only gets me into trouble. I'm looking for the music store. We have to hurry. My dad said he'll meet us by the bank in an hour."

Now Eric's eyes were closed.

"I'm imagining the ice cream," Eric said. "And it's delicious."

Eric walked into a sign.

"Excuse me," Eric said to the sign.

"Keep your eyes open and watch where you're going," Cam told him.

Cam and Eric walked past a jewelry store, a candy shop, and a pet store. Then Cam said, "There's the music store. And they're having a sale, too."

Chapter Two

Cam ran to Ernie's Everything in Music and Video store. She was about to go in when Eric yelled, "Stop! You're going in the wrong way."

Cam stopped. She looked at the gate. It was clearly marked EXIT. Near the bottom of the gate were two tiny red lights.

Cam turned around and walked back to Eric. "That gate has an alarm," Cam told Eric. "Each CD and tape in the store must have a magnetic strip on it. If you go through the gate without taking off the strip the gate beeps. When you pay, they take off the strip so you can get out without setting off the alarm."

Cam and Eric walked in through the entrance. It was a big store with lots of departments. The store was crowded with shoppers.

Cam stood by the entrance and looked around. Near the front of the store videotapes of movies and old television shows were displayed. Above them were a few television screens showing scenes from some of the tapes on sale.

Eric said, "Let's buy a movie tape."

Cam shook her head and said, "No."

"Then let's buy some blank tapes," Eric said. "We can tape television shows that are on while we're in school."

"Look," Cam said. "There's a map of the store."

Cam went to the map.

"We have to go past the movie tapes to the end of aisle seven," Cam said.

Cam started to walk away. Then she came back. She looked at the map, blinked her eyes, and said, *"Click."*

"That's in case we get lost," she told Eric. "I'll have a picture of the map stored in my head."

Cam and Eric walked down aisle seven.

Music was playing throughout the store. Then the music stopped.

"Make Ernie happy," someone announced. "Buy a CD or tape. You'll be happy, too, with Ernie's low, low prices."

10

The music started again.

"The CDs in each department are in alphabetical order," Cam told Eric.

Cam walked to the end of the aisle. Eric stopped near the middle.

Cam searched for the new Triceratops Pops CD. She couldn't find it.

"Look at this," Eric said.

He showed Cam a CD.

"It's the new Ripe Banana Band CD," Eric said. "The group's music is soft and sweet, just like a ripe banana. I love it."

Cam closed her eyes and said, *"Click."*

"I'm looking at the store map," she told Eric.

Cam opened her eyes.

"Let's try aisle four," she said.

Cam and Eric went to aisle four. But they didn't find any CDs by Triceratops Pops.

"Hm," Cam said. She put her hands on her hips and looked around.

Eric looked, too.

11

"Maybe he can help us," Eric said. "He works here."

Eric pointed to a tall young man wearing a yellow and green striped jacket. He was in aisle six next to a cart loaded with boxes. He was taking CDs from an open box and putting them on a shelf.

"Could you please tell me where to find the new Triceratops Pops CD?" Cam asked the man.

On the front of the man's jacket was a name tag that said: HELLO. I'M ERNIE'S HELPER. MY NAME IS JORDAN.

"Aisle two. Case five. Top shelf," Jordan said without turning around. "I put six discs there just a few minutes ago."

"Aisle two? Why aisle two?" Cam asked.

Jordan turned and looked down at Cam and Eric and said slowly, "Because that's where they belong."

Cam closed her eyes and said *"Click"* while she walked. Eric held her hand, so she

wouldn't walk into anyone.

"He's wrong," Cam said with her eyes still closed. "Aisle two is for Country music. Triceratops Pops is not Country."

Cam opened her eyes. She and Eric found aisle two, case five, top shelf. There was a large empty space on the shelf. But no Triceratops Pops CDs.

Chapter Three

"Maybe Jordan put them on another shelf. Maybe they're in another aisle," Eric said.

Cam closed her eyes and said, *"Click."* Then she told Eric, "There are ten music sections in this store. We've already checked Popular, New Releases, and Country. It won't take long to check the others."

Cam checked the Show Tunes section. Eric checked Jazz. Then Cam checked Classical and Rap. Eric checked Easy Listening, Rhythm and Blues, and Specialty Recordings. They didn't find the Triceratops Pops CDs.

"Let's ask Jordan," Cam said. "He put the CDs on the shelf. Maybe he can find them."

Jordan was still in aisle six. A woman was talking to him.

"I'm looking for a tape. My daughter asked me to get it for her and I said, 'That's just what I'll do.' The tape is called *Cupcake Love,* or *Cup Lake Glove,* or *Pups Above.* I'm sure you know the one I mean."

Jordan said very slowly, "I don't know what you're talking about."

The woman smiled. "I'll tell you about the people who made the tape. That's just what I'll do. It was a group called Teacher Creature or Fixture Mixture or Peach and Picture."

Jordan looked at the woman for a long while. Then he said slowly, "You want me to find a tape for you. You don't know the name of the tape and you don't know the singing group."

"That's right," the woman said.

"Well," Jordan told her, "if the tape came

out in the last five years, we probably have it. Why don't you just look at all of our eight thousand tapes until you find one that looks right."

The woman nodded her head and said, "That's just what I'll do."

As the woman walked past, Eric whispered to her, "You could call your daughter and ask her the name of the tape. There's a pay telephone right outside the store."

"Oh my yes," the woman said and smiled. "That's just what I'll do."

"Could you please help me?" Cam asked Jordan.

She told him, "We looked in aisle two, case five, top shelf for the Triceratops Pops CDs. They are not there."

"Yes they are," Jordan said. "I put them there myself."

Jordan took two CDs from the box he was still holding and put them on display.

"Please," Cam said, "could you show us where the CDs are?"

Jordan dropped the box onto the cart. He started to walk toward aisle two. As he walked, he mumbled: "Next, I'll have to show them where their pockets are so they can find their money. Then I'll have to show them the exit.

Maybe I'll even have to walk them home."

Jordan stopped. He pointed to a large 2.

"This is aisle two," he told Cam and Eric. "We keep our Country music here. Now I'll show you case five."

Jordan brought them to case five. He pointed to the top shelf and said, "And here are your CDs."

"No, they're not," Cam said.

Jordan turned. He looked on the top shelf. He looked on the other shelves, too. The CDs were gone.

"Well, this is where I put the CDs," Jordan said.

"Maybe someone stole them," Cam said.

Jordan said, "No. You can't steal from here. We have a great security system."

He thought for a moment. Then he said, "Maybe we sold all the CDs. Six is a lot to sell in just a few minutes. But this is a busy store and Triceratops Pops is a popular group. I'll check the computer."

Chapter Four

Cam and Eric followed Jordan to the end of the aisle. Jordan pressed a few buttons on the computer and then pointed to the screen.

"Do you see this? It's just like I said. We have six CDs and they haven't been sold."

"Then where are they?" Cam asked.

"Maybe someone took them off the shelf but hasn't paid for them yet. Maybe he's looking around the store for something else to buy."

"No one would buy six of the same CD,"

Cam said. "You mean six people took the T-Pops CDs off the shelf."

"So, six people are buying the discs," Jordan said as he turned and walked away. "That's possible. Ernie's Everything is a very busy store. And I have to get back to my work. I am a very busy man."

"Forget about Triceratops Pops," Eric said. "Let's get a Ripe Banana Band CD."

"No one would buy six T-Pops CDs," Cam said. "But someone might steal them from here and sell them at a flea market or yard sale."

"How would anyone get out of here with stolen CDs?" Eric asked. "They've got a security gate that beeps."

"That's a mystery," Cam said. "How did someone steal the CDs and get them past the exit gate?"

Eric clapped his hands and said, "I knew it! I just knew it! Wherever we go, you find a mystery."

Cam picked up a CD. It was in a closed plastic case. Stuck to the inside of the case was a white rectangle.

Cam showed Eric the white rectangle and said, "Here's the magnetic strip. It sets off the alarm when you leave the store."

Cam tried to open the plastic case. She couldn't.

"They open up the case and take out the CD at the register when you pay," Cam told Eric.

Cam put the CD down.

Eric hummed a tune. Then he sang softly, "Fields of green, yellow, too. I love the fields and I love you."

"Yuck! What is that?" Cam asked.

"It's a Ripe Banana song."

"Yuck," Cam said again. "It sounded more like a rotten banana song."

Cam thought for a moment. Then she leaned close to Eric and whispered, "Maybe a thief broke open the cases, took off the white rectangles, and stuffed the CDs in his shirt."

"Maybe," Eric said.

"I'll look for the broken cases," Cam told him.

Eric said, "I'll check the registers. Maybe I'll find someone buying the Triceratops Pops CDs. Maybe there's no mystery at all. You just got here too late to buy any."

Cam walked along the aisles. She looked under the tape and CD cases and behind them. She also looked at what people had in their shopping baskets.

Near the back of the store Cam felt a draft of cold air. She turned and saw that the back door was open. And there was no security gate there.

Cam was just starting toward it when she heard a loud *"Beep . . . Beep . . . Beep"* coming from the front of the store.

Chapter Five

Cam rushed down aisle six, past Jordan, to the store entrance.

Eric pointed to a man standing by the security gate. The guard opened a bag he was carrying.

Cam looked at the man. She blinked her eyes and said, *"Click."*

"This is it," the guard said as he took out a videotape rented from another store. "These always set off our alarm."

The man was about to leave.

"I'm sorry," the guard said. "I'll have to check your other bag, too."

The guard was wearing a name tag. HELLO. I'M ERNIE'S HELPER. MY NAME IS BARRY was printed on the tag.

The man with the videotape was holding another large paper shopping bag. Cam got closer to see what was in the bag.

"It's a watermelon," the man said. "I'm having a party tonight, and this will be dessert."

Barry the guard looked in the bag. Cam looked in, too. It *was* a watermelon.

"It's a big one," Barry said.

"I'm having a big party," the man told him as he left the store.

The bottom of the watermelon bag was wet and left a spot on the floor. Barry the guard wiped the floor and then went back to his seat near the cash registers.

Cam told Eric, "Come with me. I'll show you how the thief got out."

Eric followed Cam to the back door.

"There's no guard here," Cam whispered, "and there's no security gate."

Cam and Eric walked closer and looked out. The door opened out on a back street and driveway.

"Excuse me," said a woman pushing a handcart loaded with boxes. She was making a delivery.

Cam and Eric moved aside and let the woman walk past. Then they started to walk through the back door.

A tall woman wearing a yellow and green striped jacket stopped them. "This exit is for emergencies only. If you want to leave you'll have to go out the front door."

On the woman's jacket was a name tag that said: HELLO. I'M ERNIE'S HELPER. MY NAME IS SUSAN.

Cam and Eric walked away from the door.

Eric said, "Maybe the thief got out when Susan was on her lunch break."

"Sh," Cam whispered. "Look."

30

Cam pointed to a woman wearing a large raincoat. The woman was walking along the back aisle of the store.

"She's wearing a raincoat and it isn't raining," Cam whispered. "It hasn't rained all week."

Cam and Eric followed the woman. She stopped by a rack of videotapes. She took a tape from the rack and looked at it.

The woman turned and saw Cam and Eric watching her. She quickly returned the tape to the rack and walked down aisle four.

"Did you see that?" Cam asked.

"What?"

"Her pockets are full. I'll bet she's got the stolen CDs."

Eric said, "Or maybe she just has a rain hat and gloves in her pockets."

Cam and Eric walked quietly to aisle four. They stood at the end of the aisle. They pretended to be looking at the CDs. But they were really watching the woman in the raincoat.

The woman turned and saw Cam and Eric watching her. Cam smiled at the woman. Then Cam blinked her eyes and said, *"Click."*

The woman turned and walked away.

Cam whispered to Eric, "I just took a picture of her with my mental camera. I want to remember what she looks like. She might be the CD thief."

Cam and Eric walked to the end of aisle four. They looked down aisles three and five.

"Where did she go?" Cam asked.

Just then they heard a loud *"Beep . . . Beep . . . Beep."*

Chapter Six

"That's her," Cam said. "She's trying to leave the store."

Cam and Eric rushed to the front of the store. The woman in the raincoat wasn't there. Barry the guard was looking through a teenager's knapsack. He took out a bag with blank tapes that the boy had just bought at Ernie's. He took out books, papers, a lunch bag, and a videotape from the rental store.

"This is it," Barry said. "These tapes always set off our alarm."

Barry helped the boy repack his knapsack.

34

After the boy left, Cam asked the guard, "Did you see a woman wearing a raincoat walk past here?"

Cam closed her eyes and said, *"Click."*

"She has white hair and brown eyes," Cam said with her eyes still closed. "She's wearing tiny earrings, dark red lipstick, eyeglasses, sneakers, and white socks."

"I didn't see her," Barry said.

Cam opened her eyes. She leaned close to the guard and whispered, "She's wearing a raincoat and it isn't raining!"

Barry the guard leaned even closer and whispered, "I didn't see her."

Barry went back to his seat near the cash registers.

Cam said to Eric, "Then she's still here. She may be hiding from us. Or she may be in some corner taking off the magnetic strips."

Eric followed Cam past the racks of video-tapes of old movies and television shows. They walked down aisle one. Then, as they turned to walk up the next aisle, Cam stopped and pointed to a woman just ahead of them.

"She's not wearing a raincoat," Eric said. "That woman works here."

"I know she works here. She's Susan. But if Susan is in here, who's watching the back door?"

Cam and Eric went quickly to the back door. It was open.

"Maybe this is how the raincoat woman got away," Cam said as she walked through the door.

Cam and Eric were standing on a narrow driveway at the back of the mall. Trucks were parked by the back doors of some of the stores and workers were unloading the trucks. NO PARKING. LOADING ZONE was painted on many of the doors.

"I don't see her," Eric said.

Cam and Eric walked out across the driveway. They turned and looked both ways. Then, as Cam turned again and looked into the store, she saw the woman in the raincoat.

"There she is!"

Cam and Eric hurried across the driveway. But before they could get into the store Susan reached out for the door. She didn't see Cam and Eric as she pulled the door closed.

Cam tried to open the door. It was locked. She knocked and banged, but no one came to open it.

There was a large sign on the door. EMER-GENCY EXIT. PLEASE ENTER THROUGH MALL.

Cam gave the door one last knock. Then she and Eric walked around to the front. They entered the shopping mall. Someone dressed in a bear costume was about to hand Eric a flyer when Cam said, "We have no time for that."

"No, thank you," Eric said.

Eric put his hands in his pockets.

"Grrr!" the bear growled.

Cam and Eric hurried through the crowded mall to Ernie's. They were about to walk in when Cam stopped.

Cam pointed to the floor and asked, "Do you see that?"

Eric looked down at a small, wet trail.

"The thief is not in Ernie's," Cam said. "He left a long time ago."

Chapter Seven

Cam closed her eyes and said, *"Click."*

"The thief has short brown hair," Cam said with her eyes closed. "He's wearing sunglasses, a green shirt, blue pants, and sneakers."

Cam opened her eyes and said, "Let's tell the guard."

Cam and Eric went into Ernie's.

"Some CDs were stolen and we know who did it," Cam told Barry the guard.

Barry smiled. Then he turned away.

"He stole six Triceratops Pops CDs and

maybe some others, too," Cam said.

"I have a job here," Barry said. He wasn't smiling anymore. "I don't have time for children's games."

"You should listen to Cam," Eric told Barry. "She has an amazing photographic memory. She's solved lots of mysteries."

Cam closed her eyes and told Barry, "The third button on your shirt is open."

He closed the button.

"Your tie is crooked."

He straightened his necktie.

"And the number on your badge is 3640897."

"It is! You *do* have an amazing memory. Now tell me why you think some CDs were stolen from here."

Cam told Barry all about the missing discs. Then she told him about the thief. She was excited and spoke very fast.

"The CDs were taken and your gate beeped. The man was wearing sunglasses. You checked his bags and found a rented videotape and a watermelon. You should have held the tape and made him go through the gate again. It would have beeped."

Cam took a deep breath and went on.

"The bottom of the watermelon bag was wet."

"That's right," Barry said. "After he left, I wiped the floor."

Cam told Barry, "Whole watermelons are wet on the inside, not on the outside. He must have cut a hole in the side of the watermelon and hollowed it out. That's where he hid the CDs."

"What do we do now?" Barry asked.

"We look for him," Cam said. "I can give you his exact description. I have a picture of the thief stored in my head."

"Not yet," Barry said. "First I have to tell my boss that I'm leaving the store."

When Barry came back he and Eric listened as Cam described the thief. Then they went outside to search the mall.

"Look how many people there are here," Barry said. "We'll never find him."

Eric said, "He left so long ago, he's probably home already."

Cam looked at the floor. She tried to follow the trail of watermelon juice. But too many people had walked on it and too many other things had been spilt on the floor.

Barry pointed to a man wearing sunglasses and asked, "Is that him?"

"No," Cam said. "The thief is shorter and is wearing sneakers."

Barry walked slowly through the mall. Cam and Eric followed him.

"What about him?" Barry asked and pointed again.

Cam shook her head and said, "No."

By now they had walked across the mall and were standing in front of the video rental store. Eric looked at the store. Then he looked at Cam.

"We don't have to search for the thief," Eric said. "We can go to his house. I know how we can get his name, address, and probably even his telephone number."

Chapter Eight

Eric told Cam, "You just have to say *'Click.'*
Look at the picture you have in your head of
the thief and at the videotape Barry took
from his bag. The rental store can tell us who
took out that tape. And there it is, the name
of the thief."

Eric went on, "I'm sure they have his address on their computer records. They probably have his telephone number, too, his
credit card number, his date of birth, and lots
of other things about him."

Cam closed her eyes and said, *"Click."* Then she said, "He rented *Jungle Jake Returns.*"

"*Jungle Jake Returns!*" Eric asked, "Why would anyone want to watch that?"

Barry said, "He probably rented it just to fool our security system."

Cam, Eric, and Barry went into the store. Barry explained to the clerk there why they needed to know who had rented *Jungle Jake Returns.*

"I can't tell you that," the clerk said. "Our computer records are private."

"Take a look at my badge," Barry said. "I'm an Ernie's security guard. I believe the man who rented that tape is a thief."

"I can't just give you his name. I have to check first with my boss. Wait here. I'll be right back," the clerk said. Then he walked quickly to the back of the store.

"Look at all the tapes they have here," Eric said. "Some of these were in movie theaters just a few months ago."

"Ernie's has tapes, too," Barry said, "lots of tapes."

"This is where you find the most popular tapes," Cam said. She pointed to a slot in the front of the store. "People return the tapes here. As soon as the clerk checks them in, you grab them. When I come here with my parents we always look here first."

Someone outside the store dropped in a tape. It slid down a small tunnel and into a wooden box.

"There's a tape now," Cam said.

Eric looked into the box. "I saw that movie. It was good."

Another tape slid down the tunnel.

"Yuck!" Eric said. "It's an exercise tape."

Barry looked at his watch.

"I can't wait here all afternoon," Barry said.

"They sell candy here, too, and popcorn," Cam said. "I love to eat popcorn while I watch a movie."

Barry looked at his watch again.

"I'm going back there," he said. "I'll speak to his boss myself."

Just then another tape slid down the tunnel. Cam looked into the box.

"It's *Jungle Jake Returns*!"

Chapter Nine

Barry turned and ran out the door. Cam and Eric followed him.

A man wearing sunglasses, a green shirt, blue pants, and sneakers was walking from the store. When he saw Barry, Cam, and Eric coming toward him, the man started to run.

"That's him!" Cam shouted. "He's the thief."

The man was carrying a large shopping bag. He bumped into people as he ran. But he didn't stop.

Cam, Eric, and Barry were careful not to

run into people. Because they were being careful, the man was getting away.

Then the man turned to see how close they were. And he ran right into the man in the bear costume.

"Ahhh!" the man screamed when he saw the bear. He dropped the shopping bag.

"Grrr!" the bear growled.

The man grabbed at the handles of his shopping bag. But it was too late. Cam, Eric, and Barry had caught up with him.

When the man dropped the bag, the watermelon broke. Inside the bag was the broken watermelon, and lots of CDs and watches.

Barry asked, "Did you steal these watches from Benders?"

The man said, "I bought them."

"Show me the sales slip," Barry said.

The man didn't have one.

Barry held onto the man's arm and told Cam and Eric to get the police.

They found two police officers in a car

patrolling the parking lot. Cam told them about Barry, the thief, and the stolen CDs. The officers got out of their car. They followed Cam and Eric into the shopping mall and arrested the thief.

"We'll have to take the watches and CDs, too," one of the officers said. "We'll need them as evidence of the crime."

"Can't you leave just one of the Triceratops Pops CDs?" Cam asked. "That's why I went to Ernie's."

"Please," Barry said. "Leave us just one of those."

The officer gave Barry one of the Triceratops Pops CDs. Barry gave it to Cam.

"The case is sticky with watermelon juice," Barry said. "But you can wash that off. The CD inside isn't damaged."

Cam took money from her pocket and said, "I'll pay for it."

"No you won't," Barry said. "Both of you are heroes. That CD is a reward for helping

to catch the thief. Come to the store and I'm sure my boss will reward you with more CDs."

Eric asked, "Can we get a Ripe Banana Band CD?"

Barry said, "Of course."

Cam looked at Barry's watch.

"We can't go back to the store now," she said. "It's late. We have to meet my father by the bank."

"Well," Barry said, "you can come back to Ernie's anytime and claim your reward. I'll even introduce you to Ernie. He'll want to meet both of you." Barry smiled. "And don't worry. Even if you wait a long time to come back to the store, I'll remember you. I have a good memory, too."